Brick-a-Breck

Written by **Julia Donaldson**

Illustrated by Philippe Dupasquier

For Jerry - J.D

First published 2003 by
A & C Black, an imprint of Bloomsbury Publishing Plc
50 Bedford Square, London, WC1B 3DP

www.bloomsbury.com

Text copyright © 2003 Julia Donaldson
Illustrations copyright © 2003 Philippe Dupasquier

The rights of Julia Donaldson and Philippe Dupasquier to be identified as the author and
illustrator of this work respectively have been asserted by them
in accordance with the Copyrights, Designs and Patents Act 1988.

ISBN 978-0-7136-6441-6

A CIP catalogue for this book is available from the British Library.

This book is produced using paper that is made from wood
grown in managed, sustainable forests. It is natural, renewable
and recyclable. The logging and manufacturing processes conform
to the environmental regulations of the country of origin.

Printed in China by C&C Offset Printing Co Ltd, Shenzhen, Guangdong

5 7 9 10 8 6 4

Bowl One

Stephen Rice loved cereal.

This was a typical day's menu for Stephen …

Breakfast – Cracklewheat

Playground snack – Corncrunch

Packed lunch – Sunnysnaps

Teatime – Toastyoats

Suppertime – Sultana Stars

Bedtime – Choc-o-not-hoops

5

Choc-o-not-hoops? What are they? you might be wondering. Well, Stephen's mum could tell you – she worked in a cereal factory. (Lucky Stephen!)
The company that Mum worked for was called Sunfield, and their most famous cereal was called Choc-o-hoops.

Mum's job was to watch the Choc-o-hoops coming out of the machine and pick out any broken ones. She was allowed to take these ones home. They were the Choc-o-not-hoops.

The only snag about the Choc-o-not-hoops was that they didn't have a packet. Stephen loved cereal packets almost as much as the cereal itself. Sometimes they had free prehistoric pencil-tops in them.

Sometimes they had tokens to cut out, so you could save up for something really useful like a glow-in-the-dark skeleton warrior.

What's more, the packets were great
to read.

All in all, Stephen Rice was a happy
boy – until the dreadful day that Sunfield
closed down the factory where Mum
worked.

Bowl Two

Suddenly they were poor. Mum was out of a job. There were no more free Choc-o-not-hoops. In fact there wasn't any cereal, except for porridge, which didn't count.

The only way Stephen could ever eat any cereal or read any packets was to get himself invited to friends' houses.

It was at his friend Bruce's breakfast table that Stephen read about the competition. This is what he read, on the back of a packet of Choosli …

DESIGN-A-CEREAL

Sunfield are inviting you to invent your own cereal and think of a name for it. If we like the winning idea enough we'll start making it. The winner will receive a lifetime's free supply of the cereal.

There was a form for you to fill in.

Name:
Address:
Name of cereal:
Description of cereal:
Drawing of cereal:

"Can I cut this form out?" asked
Stephen.

"No, my mum won't let us till the packet's empty," said Bruce.

"That's not a problem," said Stephen, and poured himself out another bowl of Choosli. Three bowls later the packet was empty and Stephen took the form home.

Bowl Three

Stephen chewed his prehistoric pencil-top. He closed his eyes and hoped that a good idea would float into his mind. It didn't.

"Ricy Robots … Brontosaurus Bran …"

"Too difficult to make," said his mum, who was a bit of an expert.

"Snowflakes," he murmured.
"That sounds like a washing powder,"
said Bruce, who had come to tea.
"Well, you think of something, then,"
said Stephen.

But Bruce just suggested silly things like
Soggylumps and Grottygrain.

The closing date for the competition drew near. Two days before it, Stephen went to his school's Summer Fair. He spent most of his pocket money on Fibreflake flapjacks and was just nibbling one when Mum appeared, clutching a purple vase.

"What a colour!" said Stephen. "Did you fish it out of a trough of Ribena?" "No," said Mum. "I bought it at the bric-a-brac stall."

Then, "What's the matter?" she asked, for Stephen was punching the air as if he'd scored a goal.

"That's it!" he said. "Brick-a-Breck!"

Bowl Four

Stephen's mum sat in front of the television. The presenter of *Kidsnews* was talking.

"Eight-year-old Stephen Rice heard this week that he is the winner of Sunfield's Design-a-Cereal competition. Can you tell us about Brick-a-Breck, Stephen?"

"Yes. They're shaped like little bricks," said Stephen. "So you can build things with them before you eat them. Like this." He held up a picture. A cereal bowl with a castle in it filled the screen.

"Well," said the presenter, "Sunfield liked Stephen's idea so much that they've actually made some sample Brick-a Brecks – or should I say Breck-a-Bricks? – and here's Stephen with another idea."

Stephen appeared again with a bowl in which was an igloo made of cereal bricks. "These bricks are white because they're coconut-coated," he said, "so I thought an igloo would be a good idea."

"And what's the next step, Stephen?"

"Destruction," said Stephen, brandishing a milk jug. He poured milk on to the igloo and it collapsed. Stephen was getting rather carried away. Some of the milk splashed the presenter's tie.

"But aren't you sad to see your work destroyed?" asked the presenter.

"Oh no," said Stephen. "I just love eating cereal, you see," and he started tucking into the collapsed igloo.

"Stephen Rice, thank you very much," said the presenter, wiping his tie. "And now on to the Brazilian rainforest …"

Bowl Five

Stephen's mum wasn't the only person watching *Kidsnews*. A man called Jasper saw it too. Jasper was the director of a film company which had been hired to make a TV commercial advertising Brick-a-Breck.

"That's the boy! He'll be perfect!" cried Jasper when he saw Stephen waving his spoon about.

And that was why a month later Stephen and his pretend sister were sitting at a breakfast table in a television studio. The pretend sister was a rather annoying girl called Clare.

"What other commercials have you been in?" she asked. "None," said Stephen.

"I have," said Clare. "I've been in Supersoup and Great Big Softy toilet paper. This one's going to be easy peasy Japanesy."

It did sound quite simple. The children had to pour milk on a Brick-a-Breck castle and ship and then eat them, while a little muscle-man made of Brick-a-Breck did press-ups and danced on the table.

The script was:

Clare: *Castle–ruin*

Stephen: *Ship–wreck*

Brick-a-Breck man: *Build 'em up with Brick-a-Breck!*

There was a lot of bustle in the television studio. Some people were scurrying around arranging things on the table, while others fiddled about with the big bright lamps.

Stephen was getting fidgety. This was taking ages. Even though he had eaten a fair bit of Brick-a-Breck during the rehearsal, he was beginning to feel hungry again.

At last Jasper was ready for Take One. A girl clapped a clapperboard.

Brick-a-Breck
Take 1

Clare, smiling sweetly, placed the last brick on her Brick-a-Breck castle and said, "Castle."

Then she picked up the milk jug, poured milk on it and said, "Ruin."

29

Now it was Stephen's turn. He placed the
last brick on his ship and said, "Ship,"
then poured milk on it and said, "Wreck,"
as it collapsed.

After that, both children picked up their
spoons and started to eat the cereal from
their bowls.

"Cut," said Jasper.

Clare put down her spoon but Stephen finished eating his shipwreck. It was delicious.

Everyone else was crowding round a television, ready to see how Take One had turned out. Stephen joined them. One thing was puzzling him. "Where's the Brick-a-Breck man?" he asked.

"Don't be silly," said Clare. "He's a cartoon – they add him later."

Otherwise, everything looked fine to Stephen, but Jasper wasn't happy. "We need more shine on the orange juice," he said.

So a lighting man made one of the lights brighter, while the props people rearranged the milk jug and cereal packet and brought a brand new castle and ship to the table.

"Take Two," said Jasper, and they went through it all again.

Afterwards, when Stephen had eaten up the shipwreck plus Clare's ruined castle which she didn't want, he joined the others round the television screen.

"Heaven," said Jasper as his eyes lit on the gleaming orange juice, but as soon as Stephen's face appeared he put his hand to his head. "That nose won't do," he said.

Clare giggled rudely.

"Too much shine," said Jasper.
Apparently, the light which had made
the orange juice shine so brightly had had
the same effect on Stephen's nose.
Stephen sighed as the make-up lady
dabbed his nose with a powder puff.

"What about Clare?" he asked.
"I'm not a red-nosed reindeer like you,"
said Clare. Stephen was getting fed up
with her. He hoped Take Three would
be the last.

Bowl Six

Two hours later, Stephen was hoping
Take Fourteen would be the last. This is
what had happened …

Take Three:
Stephen knocked the
cereal packet over.

Take Four:
A man from Sunfield arrived
late and said there should
be a bowl of fruit on the
table to give a more
healthy look.

Take Five:
The grapes
didn't look
shiny enough.

Take Six:
Someone said the purple grapes didn't go
with Stephen's red T-shirt. Some green
grapes were found instead.

Take Seven:
Stephen's ship
collapsed before
he had poured
the milk on to it.

Take Eight:
Clare wasn't
smiling enough.
(Stephen was
pleased that
she had done
something
wrong at last.)

Take Nine:
Clare kicked
Stephen under the
table and some of
the milk splashed
into the fruit bowl.

Take Ten:
Jasper said
the table looked too
crowded and decided to
remove the orange juice.

Take Eleven:
The man from Sunfield
said he wanted the
orange juice back
and that it would be
all right not to have
the fruit bowl after all.

Take Twelve:
Stephen
wasn't looking
happy enough
while eating
the cereal.

Take Thirteen:
Stephen wasn't looking rosy enough –
in fact, he was looking slightly green.
Jasper got the make-up lady to rub
some red stuff on his cheeks.

"I think they should have got Simeon Jay
to act your part," Clare told Stephen.
"He was in Great Big Softy toilet paper
with me and he was brilliant."

Just at that moment, Stephen wished that Simeon Jay, or anyone, could take his place. There was a reason for his greenness: he had eaten a whole fleet of Brick-a-Breck ships and was feeling sick – or seasick, maybe. His stomach, which Mum always called a bottomless pit, now felt more like a stormy sea.

"Take Fourteen," said Jasper.

As Clare did her bit, the storm in Stephen's stomach grew stronger. He placed the last brick on the ship, smiled as brightly as he could, and picked up the milk jug for the fourteenth time. Just then, his stomach gave a gigantic heave, and instead of pouring milk on to his ship, Stephen was sick all over it.

There were no more "takes", except
for taking Stephen home.

In the studio, Jasper asked to see
Take Two again – the one in which
Stephen's nose had been too shiny.
This time, Jasper said, "I like that
shine! It's healthy, it's natural, it spells
childhood! That's the one!"

Bowl Seven

Brick-a-Breck was a big success. Shops, cereal bowls and tummies all over the country were full of it.

This was such good news for Sunfield that they were able to re-open the factory in Stephen's town and give his mum her job back.

Actually, it isn't quite the same job. Instead of checking Choc-o-hoops she has to check Brick-a-Brecks, and make sure they are all properly brick-shaped.

This means that instead of bringing back bags of Choc-o-not-hoops she could bring back bags of Breck-a-not-bricks. But she doesn't … because Stephen, as the winner of the competition, receives a lifetime's free supply.

For some reason, though, Stephen has gone off Brick-a-Breck. In fact, he has gone off cereal altogether …

His latest craze is for pasta – shells, quills, tubes, spirals, he loves them all.

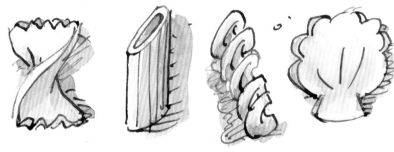

At this very moment, Stephen is poring over a packet of Romeo's Pasta Ribbons and reading aloud …